David's Journey
on the
Underground Railroad

by Linda Sibley

Perfection Learning®

Cover Illustration: Dea Marks

Inside Illustration: Dea Marks

For my family

About the Author

Linda Sibley has lived in Harlingen, Texas, her entire life, except for one year away at school. She now lives there with her husband, Rick, and two children, Jeremy and Jennifer.

Ms. Sibley did contract work for attorneys for 15 years so she could be at home to raise her children. Now she is working at a local hospital part-time. This enables her to spend time writing, which is her favorite thing to do. She also enjoys reading and searching for interesting antiques.

Traveling is another of Ms. Sibley's interests. So far she has visited 24 states and 2 countries. She is always looking for an excuse to go on another trip.

Printed in the United States of America. For information, contact

Perfection Learning® Corporation

1000 North Second Avenue, P.O. Box 500

Logan, Iowa 51546-0500.

Phone: 1-800-831-4190 • Fax: 1-712-644-2392

Cover Craft® ISBN-13: 978-0-7569-0076-2

Cover Craft® ISBN-10: 0-7569-0076-x

Paperback ISBN-13: 978-0-7891-5432-3

Paperback ISBN-10: 0-7891-5432-3

4 5 6 7 8 9 PP 12 11 10 09 08 07

Printed in the U.S.A.

Contents

1

A New Adventure

I'd been staring at the clock on the wall all afternoon. It should have been 3:00 a long time ago. I was just thinking about throwing a book at the bell when it finally rang. Ah . . . what a beautiful sound! Christmas vacation had officially begun.

Grabbing my coat, I was out the door in a flash. I expertly dodged other students. They were as anxious as I was to be free for the next 14 days.

Overall, this had been a pretty good semester for me. My parents were pleased with my grades. I was pleased with my football season. I had scored two touchdowns in the play-off game. It didn't even matter so much that we had lost. I had still been the talk of the school for weeks after that game.

I ran the whole five blocks home. To add a little challenge, I jumped a fire hydrant, Mrs. Franklin's bush, and a wooden fence.

No one was home yet. I went straight to my room. I dropped my coat just inside the door.

I never bother untying my shoes. It only wastes time. So I caught the back of my heel with the toe of the other shoe. Then I pulled off the heel and kicked it across the room. I aimed a little more carefully with the second shoe. It landed neatly in the trash can. Oh, yes, life was good.

I heard the front door slam. Jenny's footsteps thudded up the stairs. Every day I count to ten. Ten steps and she would be popping into my room. Then she'd talk excitedly about her day. That was the thing I liked most about my little sister. She was always happy. Well, she was *almost* always happy.

"Hey, David," she called as she plopped on my bed. Each day she took one long breath. Then she started with a story about her day.

"Remember that new guy in my class named Chester?" she began. She did not let me answer. She *never* let me answer.

"Well, he blew up a computer today. We still don't know exactly what he did to it. First there was a loud pop. Then black smoke came pouring out of it. It was pretty funny. You should have seen Mr. Simpson's face," she said, laughing. "Don't you wish you'd been there?"

Again I had no chance to answer before she continued. She was still chattering when Mom and Dad came into my room.

I like that about my room. It seems to be a gathering place for the whole family. Dad and I usually stretch out across the floor. Mom and Jenny sit cross-legged on my bed.

Jenny and I would tell about any interesting things that happened at school that day. Mom would relate stories about the college history class she teaches. I am always amazed that even college kids do dumb things. Dad is the high school football coach. He always has funny stories to tell about the team.

Today, however, the topic was what we would be doing during Christmas vacation. Instead of stretching lazily across the floor, Dad sat in the chair at my desk. That always means that he has something serious to talk about.

"We need to talk over our plans again," he said firmly. "I'm not sure that you kids realize how dangerous this trip could be."

"He's right," Mom added. "Finding the time machine that Grandpa invented was a wonderful gift. But we have to be careful to use it wisely. Our trip to 1880 last summer was a success. But you have to realize the difference in traveling back to 1853. This was a time when African Americans were held as slaves. Once we return there, we will be in great danger.

"We still plan to arrive in Ripley, Ohio," she continued. "It was a town that hated slavery. There were people throughout the town that worked to hide runaway slaves. We believe it would be the safest place for us."

"What your mother is trying to say," said Dad solemnly, "is that once we arrive, we will be in grave danger because of the color of our skin. We could be captured and taken away as slaves ourselves."

There was a long, heavy silence in the room.

"Like I told you before," I said, "I understand that it's dangerous. But I still want to go and try to help."

"Me too," Jenny said.

"We're very torn over what to do," Mom said. "Your father and I have talked about this for a long time. We feel it's something we have to do. We would hate to leave you both behind. But we're scared to take you with us too. We just don't know what to do."

I sat on the bed next to Mom. I put my arm around her shoulders.

"It's going to be okay, Mom," I reassured her. "We'll be very careful. I promise."

There was silence in the room as everyone considered the dangers.

After a while, I said with determination, "I think if it's too dangerous for Jenny and me, then it's too dangerous for you and Dad."

"Yeah, that's right," Jenny chimed in.

With that, I stood up in the middle of the room.

"I say the Smithers family sticks together all the way," I declared.

I extended my right arm with my hand down. Jenny stood and put her hand over mine.

"Okay, son. I think you may be right," agreed Dad. He smiled as he stood and placed his hand over Jenny's. We watched Mom as she slowly stood. She quietly placed her hand over Dad's.

"All for one and one for all," I said, smiling.

"You're right," Mom said. "We Smithers stick together!"

That's when I knew the final decision had been made. We would be traveling to Ripley, Ohio. We planned to arrive in December of 1853. We would have just 11 days to try to make our contribution to the Underground Railroad.

2

The Departure

We spent the next day getting everything ready to go. We gathered our clothes from our last trip. Then we added some long johns, wool coats, and gloves.

We went to Grandma's first thing on Sunday morning. We decided to have an early Christmas with her before we left on our trip. We had quite a load with our clothes and all the presents.

I could smell the turkey cooking as we opened the front door.

"Merry Christmas!" Jenny called to Grandma, who was busy in the kitchen.

"Merry Christmas to you," she said brightly. She stuck her head around the corner. "My goodness, look at the presents!" she exclaimed.

"And we've got more in the car," laughed Jenny.

Jenny and I stacked the presents under the tree. Then we insisted on opening them right away. I had asked for only two special things this year. I was hoping I would get them both.

The more expensive one was a DVD player. My best friends, Jeff and Ryan, were both getting one for Christmas. I thought it was important that I have one too.

The other thing I wanted was a chemistry kit. I thought it would be cool to mix up chemicals and see what happened.

I unwrapped my first present. It was the DVD player I'd wanted. I was even more pleased when I unwrapped the second package. It was a chemistry kit with tons of test tubes, chemical packets, and other lab equipment. There were other presents too—movies, CDs, and clothes.

"Okay, Jenny," I said contentedly after I'd

opened the last one. "It's your turn."

I handed her one of her gifts.

"Let me have the other one," she demanded. "I want to open the art set first."

We all turned and looked at her. Her smile faded as she realized what she'd said.

"Well, young lady," said Mom sternly. "Just how do you know that's an art set?"

"I . . . uh . . . uh . . ." she stammered.

"You've been peeking at your presents again, haven't you?" Dad asked.

"Well, yes," she said slowly. "I can't help it. I just can't wait until Christmas. I just *have* to see what they are."

She looked at Mom and Dad. She waited to see how mad they were.

"I guess I'll have to figure out a better place to hide your presents from now on," Mom said. She was smiling, so Jenny figured she was off the hook.

Relieved, Jenny ripped off the paper. It was a deluxe art set complete with paints, markers, colored pencils, sketch pads, and a canvas. She was thrilled! At the age of eight, she already thought she would be a brilliant artist someday.

Jenny opened her next gifts quickly. Her face showed no surprise. It was obvious that she already knew the contents of each one.

After all the presents were opened, Dad and I went out to check on the time machine. It had remained untouched in the garage since last summer. We marveled at Grandpa's handiwork again as we admired his magnificent invention.

Inside, the control panel was as impressive as a jetliner's. We cleaned the giant capsule. We polished the clear glass window. Then we buffed the shiny stainless steel ends. We made sure everything was in place for the trip.

When we were sure that everything was set, we went back inside. Everyone gathered at the table to eat Christmas dinner. Dad said the blessing. He added a special request for our safety on the trip.

After dinner, we layered on all of our clothes. We were not going to be able to carry much with us. We entered the time machine and settled in.

Dad set the dials to travel to Ripley, Ohio. It was now 7:00 p.m. We were to arrive at that time on December 20, 1853. We were to return on December 30 from exactly the same spot where we had arrived.

Dad turned the final dial. We waved to Grandma and were gone in an instant. Once again that dizzying journey began. I felt the familiar roller coaster ride. Pictures flashed rapidly around me. I could catch pieces of conversation, but I couldn't put the words together to make any sense. Suddenly, as quickly as it had begun, it stopped.

Immediately, I felt the sting of cold air. We found ourselves standing outside on a dark, cold night. The wind was howling around us. We quickly pulled our coats tighter and huddled together.

"It's so cold!" Jenny yelled over the raging wind.

"We need to find a warm place quickly!" shouted Mom.

"Remember, we're looking for a house with a lantern in the window," Dad called. He stepped out of the huddle to survey our surroundings. "The light is the signal that it's a safe house."

Our hopes sank as we looked around and discovered there were only two houses. Both of them were completely dark. We stood there on the snow-covered ground. We were shivering and didn't know what to do next.

"Listen!" Mom said sharply. "I think I hear horses."

"Hide yourselves!" yelled Dad.

He grabbed Mom and Jenny and pushed them into the darkness behind a clump of trees. He shouted for me to follow. I just had time to get behind a big oak tree before two horses pounded past me.

The riders jumped down from their horses. They shouted as they walked to the first house. They beat on the door loudly and called for someone to open up.

"Open that door right now!" hollered one of the men. His voice was full of rage. "I know you're hiding them in there!"

"Send them out here right now, and we won't hurt you," the other man roared. "But we aren't leaving until you open this door."

After several more minutes of pounding, the door slowly opened. An elderly woman stood in the doorway. She was wrapped in a shawl and holding a lantern.

"What do you want? Why are you beating on an old lady's door in the middle of the night?" she asked, looking small and helpless.

"I have four slaves that ran away. I heard they were headed this way," the man answered. "If you're hiding them, you'd better send them on out. I don't mean you any harm. But I aim to collect what I own."

"There isn't anyone hiding in my house," she said, coughing from the cold air.

"I don't believe you, old woman!" he bellowed. "And I'm not leaving here until I know for sure."

The men pushed their way through the door. We could hear them stomping through the house and shouting. After a few minutes, they hurried out of the house. They slammed the door behind them.

"I'm going to the next house!" yelled one of the men. "You go around back and see if you can find any sign of them."

My heart beat wildly as I watched the two men search frantically for any runaway slaves. I couldn't see Mom and Dad from where I was hiding. Suddenly I felt very alone and scared.

One man banged loudly on the door of the next house. He shouted over and over. But no one ever came to the door.

Finally, the men seemed satisfied. They jumped onto their horses and rode off into the darkness.

We waited a few minutes after they were gone. Then we dared to move from our hiding places. I could see the fear in Jenny's eyes. Her hand trembled as she reached for mine.

"What are we going to do?" Mom asked nervously.

"I don't know," said Dad. He pulled his collar up to protect his face from the cold wind. "We may have to start searching for shelter somewhere else."

"Dad!" Jenny said excitedly. "Look at the window!"

I turned to look. A lantern had been placed in the window of the first house. The glow from that lantern was a beautiful sight!

3

The Passengers

"Let's go!" Jenny called as she started toward the house. "That has to be a safe house."

"Wait!" Dad said. He grabbed her arm and pulled her back. "I want all of you to wait here and stay hidden. I'll go to the door first to make sure it's safe."

"Be careful, Tom," Mom pleaded.

We watched as he disappeared around to the back of the house. It seemed like forever before he reappeared and waved for us to join him.

"She says we're welcome to stay," Dad whispered softly. He held the back door open for us.

The warmth of that little kitchen felt wonderful as we stole quietly into the house. The old woman standing there looked tired and sick.

"I've been expecting you," she said. She motioned us through the house. "I have a warm place fixed for you in the cellar."

She carried a candle and shielded its flame with her hand. She led us through the darkened house. We followed her down the stairs into the cellar.

"I don't understand what you mean about 'expecting us,' " Mom said as we gathered in the cellar.

"I got a wire from Tennessee that you-all were on your way," she said. "Aren't you the Douglas family?"

"No, we're not," said Mom, hesitating. "We're the Smithers."

"You mean I'm going to get two runaway families in one night?" she asked.

"Actually, we're not runaways," started Dad. He told her the story that we had rehearsed before leaving home. "We've come from Pennsylvania where we were born free. We came here because we want to help in any way we can."

"You were born free in the North, but you came south to help runaways?" she asked in amazement.

"That's right," Mom replied.

"Well, if that don't beat all," she said. She shook her head in wonder.

Then she looked Mom straight in the eye. She said grimly, "You do know that you're in as much danger as the runaways? The slave hunters comb all the land alongside the Ohio River. They're always searching for runaways. They're not going to care if you were born free or not."

"Yes, we know," Mom answered. "But we came anyway."

After a moment, the woman's face broke into a smile. She said, "My name's Mayme Marie Taylor. You can call me Mayme. I've been helping runaways for almost three years now.

"I reckon there's another family coming here tonight," she added. "I'd better be getting back upstairs to watch for them."

Mayme turned toward the stairs. She stopped in a fit of coughing. We watched her silently as she struggled to control her breathing. Finally she took a deep breath, and the coughing stopped.

"Are you okay?" Mom asked.

"Yes, I'll be fine," Mayme said, facing us again. "I've had this pesky cough for weeks. I can't seem to shake it.

"Now you folks settle in," she continued. She set the candle on an old wooden box. "There's a stack of quilts in here. I'll fetch you some food in a little while."

"There's no need to worry about food for us," Mom said quickly. "We ate just a short time ago."

"Suit yourselves," Mayme said. She made her way up the stairs slowly.

We grabbed some quilts and huddled together on the earthen floor. I was beginning to have doubts that we were going to be able to help anyone. I was afraid we were going to freeze to death on the first night!

A few hours later, Mayme opened the cellar door again. Through the dim light of the candles, I could make out several dark figures.

"These are the others I was expecting," she announced. "It appears that Mr. Douglas is not traveling with them. This is Charity Douglas and her children, Peter, Nate, and Liza."

When I saw them, I was shocked by their sad condition. I had never seen anyone looking so weary and pitiful. Their clothes were worn thin. There was little to keep them warm in the winter winds and snow.

Little Liza could not have been more than three years old. She clutched tightly to her mother's neck. Exhaustion filled Mrs. Douglas's face. I knew she must have been carrying Liza all day.

The older boy named Peter looked to be about 12. I wondered why he was carrying Nate. Nate was big enough to be walking by himself. He must have been at least six.

Peter never put Nate down either. He held him protectively even after they entered the room.

Mayme and Mom began to wrap quilts around the family's shoulders. Mrs. Douglas smiled gratefully.

"Please sit down," Dad said. "We have a warm spot here."

Mrs. Douglas dropped quickly to the floor. She still clung tightly to the little girl. Mayme was already shuffling back up the stairs. She said she would be back shortly with some hot soup.

Peter carefully sat his little brother down next to his mother and wrapped him in a quilt. Peter looked as exhausted as his mother. He only mumbled a soft hello.

Mom and Dad quickly made friends with Mrs. Douglas. She began to tell her story.

She and her husband, Percy, had been slaves on the same plantation in Tennessee. Six months ago, their owner had sold Percy to another man in Kentucky. Percy had been beaten and treated badly by his new master. Finally, he had run away. He'd crossed the Ohio River and made it to Cincinnati. He had gotten word to Mrs. Douglas about where he was hiding. They planned to meet in Cincinnati and then go on north to Canada together.

"And you've made it all this way, just you and the children?" Mom asked.

"We walked all the way," Mrs. Douglas said proudly. "And we're going to walk all the way to Cincinnati if we have to."

"That's incredible," Dad declared.

"We aren't any different from anyone else who wants freedom," she said. "I suppose that's why you're here too."

"We're from Pennsylvania." Dad started telling our prepared story. "Annie and I were born free.

We've been very blessed. Now we want to help someone else."

"You were safe in the North? Then you came to the South to help somebody else get free?" Mrs. Douglas asked. She looked as surprised as Mayme had.

"That's right," said Mom firmly.

"Glory be!" Mrs. Douglas exclaimed.

Mayme brought steaming hot bowls of soup. The Douglas family ate hungrily. Mayme stayed and talked with us.

"Your family is welcome to stay here as long as need be," she said to Mom and Dad. "Bill Lankton is normally the conductor from here to Cincinnati, but he broke his leg. I'll be taking Mrs. Douglas and her children to Cincinnati."

"You're taking them by yourself?" asked Dad in surprise.

"I've made the trip before. I know the way. There's nothing to worry about," she assured him.

"But you're sick!" exclaimed Mom. "You'll never last in the cold."

"I'll be all right," Mayme protested. "It'll only take me about a week to make the trip."

"I think Annie is right," Dad joined in. "I can tell by looking at you that you've been sick for a while. You can't trudge across Ohio in the snow!"

"We'll go by ourselves if we have to," said Mrs. Douglas. "We're supposed to meet Percy in Cincinnati the day after Christmas. There isn't anything that will keep us from making it on time."

Dad and Mom were looking at Jenny and me. We all knew this was our chance to help. They searched our faces for our answer. Jenny and I nodded quietly.

"We can do it," declared Dad. "We'd be glad to take the Douglas family to Cincinnati."

"Oh, no," protested Mayme. "You don't even know the way."

"I know that I can follow the Ohio River. It will take me right to Cincinnati," he argued.

"But you're going to have to go north a bit and then swing around to Cincinnati. Otherwise, you're going to run into slave hunters all along the river," Mayme countered.

"Okay," offered Dad. "You tell me the way you would go."

Mayme still hesitated. Finally, she looked as if she'd made up her mind. She brought out an old weathered map. The adults gathered in the candlelight to study a route. After a short time, they agreed on the safest course. They made plans to leave the next day.

"We'll finish up in the morning," Mayme announced suddenly. "I know you folks must be mighty tired."

She covered Mrs. Douglas and Liza with an extra quilt. Then she blew out the candle and left the cellar pitch dark. We heard her making her way up the stairs in the dark.

My mind began to wander as I thought of the journey ahead of us. Traveling for a week in this cold weather sounded miserable! This had been such an easy decision to make when I was back home. Then I had been warm and comfortable in my bedroom.

I was beginning to worry about Jenny. She had sat pressed to my side the whole time. She hadn't spoken a word. It was unusual not knowing exactly what was on her mind. She never thought twice about telling me everything back home.

"Are you all right?" I whispered to her quietly.

"Yeah, I'm just cold," she answered. Her voice quivered.

I straightened the quilt around her shoulders and pulled her closer. There was so much on my mind. I couldn't go to sleep for a long time. I lay huddled next to Jenny, sharing her warmth.

I kept trying to put myself in Peter's place. I wondered what his life must be like. In my mind, I could still see his dark eyes staring at me. They were filled with such a deep sadness. I shivered at the thought of what might have put it there.

4

All Aboard

When I awoke the next morning, I had no idea what time it was. Dad and Mom were the only ones awake. They were studying the map again and whispering quietly.

I watched them as they worked. I realized how proud I was of them. Not many parents would ever attempt anything like this.

They had managed to light the candle. The flame danced about, casting the only light in the cellar.

Everyone was waking up as Mayme came with breakfast.

"I'm afraid you're going to have to delay leaving until this evening," she announced. "It's a beautiful day outside. There's not a cloud in the sky. The trouble is you'd be spotted in a minute on such a clear day. The sun will help, though, because it'll melt some of the snow. You won't have to fret about leaving tracks in fresh snow."

"We'd best be leaving before evening!" Mrs. Douglas protested. "We have to get to Cincinnati!"

"It'll be all right," Dad assured her. "I give you my word that we'll be there on time."

Mrs. Douglas seemed to relax a little. Everyone went to work on flapjacks and maple syrup. After breakfast, Mayme came in with an armful of clothes for the Douglas family.

"We ran with nothing but the clothes on our backs," explained Mrs. Douglas.

"I've got plenty, so don't you worry," said Mayme generously. She was able to supply them all with coats and shoes. Little Liza laughed and danced in circles, showing off her new clothes.

Mayme handed Nate a coat. He touched it gently, as if he'd never seen anything like it before. When she handed him shoes, he smiled broadly. He lunged forward to grab them from her hands.

"Mama!" he exclaimed. "I have shoes. I can walk now."

Sadness showed in Mrs. Douglas's eyes. I wondered why. Then Nate jerked off the quilt to put on his new shoes. Both of his feet were twisted inward. That's why Peter had been carrying Nate. Nate wasn't able to walk.

Peter hesitated. Then he took the shoes from Nate. They were a little big. They slipped easily over his clumsy feet.

"I want to walk now, Peter," Nate said. "Help me up."

Peter helped Nate to his feet. Nate struggled to put one foot in front of the other. Frustrated and close to tears, Nate plopped back down.

"I can't," he said through his tears. "I still can't walk, Peter."

"You don't need to walk today," Peter consoled him. "We're going to stay here and rest until tonight. It doesn't matter anyway because I'll carry you. And think how warm your feet are going to be with those new shoes."

Nate brightened at this. He seemed satisfied as his brother covered his legs with a quilt. Peter left the new shoes uncovered for Nate to admire.

We spent the day restlessly waiting to get on our way. Jenny made friends with Liza. She played with her and tried to teach her a song.

Peter, however, stayed by Nate's side. He clearly wanted nothing to do with me. I knew that yesterday Peter had been tired. But today he acted as if he were angry with me. I didn't understand it.

After a hearty meal, we prepared to leave. Mayme packed some food for our trip. We again layered on every piece of clothing we had to prepare for the cold. I was starting to get excited again. Last night's worries had faded.

It was dark when we stepped out the back door. Liza was allowing Dad to carry her for now. That gave Mrs. Douglas a break. Peter, however, had refused offers to help carry Nate.

We formed a single line. We quietly worked our way through the woods with Dad in the lead. There was only a quarter moon that provided a little light. We stayed close together. We listened for one another's boots as they softly crunched the snow.

Jenny stepped back in line right after we started and took my hand. She wanted to walk together. That was okay with me. As we ducked below a low-hanging limb, an owl hooted loudly. Jenny jumped back so hard that she pulled me down in the snow.

"It's just an owl, Jenny," I said. I brushed the snow off me.

"I know," she said, flustered. "It just scared me."

"No talking," Mom whispered sternly over her shoulder.

We continued in silence for hours. Even little Liza made no sound. She seemed to sense the danger even at such a young age.

We stopped only twice all night to rest. We pushed ourselves to keep walking. When it was near sunrise, we discovered a cave. Dad decided that it would be a safe place to hide during the day.

At that point, I didn't care *where* we stopped. I just wanted to stop so I could sit down awhile. At first my feet had ached from the cold. Now they were just numb. I began to imagine having my toes cut off as a result of frostbite.

We huddled together in the cave. We didn't dare start a fire for fear we would be discovered. We slept only a couple of hours before Dad insisted we needed to find better shelter. It had turned dark and cloudy. The air smelled of a coming storm.

As we continued walking, the sky grew darker and darker. It became difficult to walk against the force of the wind. We struggled on, desperate to find a refuge from the storm.

"Listen," Mom said. She stopped in her tracks. "I hear a bell."

"It's a church bell," agreed Mrs. Douglas. "We're near a town."

Dad made us stay hidden while he went ahead to check.

"It's a town all right," he reported when he returned. "Mayme said to always watch for a lantern in a window. But the only lantern I see is in the church window. Do you think it's a station for the Underground Railroad?"

"I don't know," replied Mom. "But I know we've got to try. We can't stay out here any longer."

To my surprise, Dad insisted I come with him to check out the church. As we walked, Dad put his arm around me and pulled me close.

"David," he said quietly. "I'm going to knock on the door. I want you to wait at the side of the building. Be prepared in case something happens to me. I need to know that you can stand in for me and keep everyone safe. Can I count on you, David?"

I swallowed hard and answered, "Yes, Dad. You can count on me."

5

Danger, Danger Everywhere

I stood in the shadows and watched Dad knock softly. After a long while, we could hear steps approaching the door.

"Who's there?" came a gruff voice.

Dad used the code that Mayme had taught us. "A friend of a friend," he answered.

Immediately the door opened. "Come in quickly," the man said. "Are there more of you?"

"There are eight all together," Dad answered.

"Bring them in from the cold," the man invited.

He led us to a small room in the back of the church. In the middle of the room sat a big black potbellied stove. What a welcome sight that was! I was thrilled to see anything that would provide some heat for my tired, aching body. Soon a fire was blazing. We moved as close to the heat as we dared.

Reverend Sumpter alerted his family to our arrival. They provided us with blankets and hot food. Much to my surprise, I soon found myself scarfing down cabbage soup. This was something I would never have dared try before. It wasn't that I was really picky about what I ate. But I'd pick pizza over cabbage soup any day.

The reverend stood up. He said he was going out for more wood. Peter offered to go instead.

"No, son," insisted his mother. "It's too dangerous."

"I can take care of myself," he replied sharply.

"I'll go too," I said. I was anxious to do something to help.

"I don't need you," Peter snorted.

I hesitated a moment but decided to go anyway. I felt safe in the darkness. There were only a few pieces of wood already cut. Peter pulled the ax out of the splitting log and quickly went to work. He had the strength of a grown man as he expertly split the logs. Without saying a word, he picked up an armload of wood and carried it into the church.

He had not challenged me verbally. But I felt as if I had been challenged in some way. I decided to accept.

Setting a log on its end, I lowered the ax with all my might. It fell right into the center of the log, wedging itself tightly. I struggled and struggled to release the ax. All the while, I thought about how ridiculous I must look. Finally, I gave up. I picked up the rest of the cut wood and went inside where it was warm. I had just joined the others when we heard a terrible racket.

Quickly the reverend threw back a rug on the floor. A trapdoor lay beneath. He jerked up the door. Below was a small, dark room.

"Get in! Get in!" he insisted.

We had barely entered the little room before the trapdoor slammed over our heads. We sat in the dark, close quarters, listening for any sounds above us. We heard the chairs being moved about. Footsteps creaked on the wooden floor. Then there was silence.

I felt Liza begin to squirm. Mrs. Douglas struggled to quiet her. I was pressed close to Nate and Peter. I could feel Nate shiver as he clung to Peter. Then suddenly we heard footsteps right above us and loud voices arguing.

"You've got runaways in here! I know you do. So don't you tell me you don't!" someone shouted loudly.

We listened as the reverend answered calmly. "Well, sir, you can see for yourself that there are no runaways in this room."

"I heard somebody out back cutting wood. I know it wasn't you, old man!" he yelled. "Tell me where they went!"

There was silence again. We imagined the reverend was refusing to speak.

There was a loud thud. Something heavy hit the floor above us. Jenny covered her mouth with her hands, forcing back a scream. We continued to listen as the voices and footsteps disappeared. We waited, wondering what to do.

Soon we began to hear voices again. We recognized them as the reverend's family. When the trapdoor was raised, Mrs. Sumpter was standing above us.

"You can come out now," she said. "They're gone."

As we climbed out, we saw the reverend slumped in a chair. He was holding a bloodstained towel to his head.

"We're so sorry," Mom said sadly. "We never wanted this to happen."

"I'm going to be fine," assured the reverend. He was still wiping blood from the gash in his forehead. "It's not the first time I've had to deal with that sorry lot of men."

"We know they're going to come knocking sometimes," his wife agreed. "We expect it."

"I've never seen white folks who were willing to give up their lives for a slave," said Mrs. Douglas. She shook her head slowly in wonder. "Now I've seen it two times—you folks and Mayme Taylor."

"Not all white people think alike," said the reverend. "Some of us believe that everyone was created equal, regardless of skin color. Any runaway who seeks refuge in my church is going to find it!"

"I'm grateful to you, sir," said Mrs. Douglas.

"We are also thankful for your kindness," added Dad.

"And I'm especially grateful for the cabbage soup!" I exclaimed.

Everyone broke into laughter. I was glad that I could say something to break up the serious mood.

Mrs. Sumpter and her daughters worked to make us comfortable around the warm stove. I wrapped myself in a quilt. Then I found a place on the floor between Dad and Jenny.

A week ago, I would have had plenty of complaints about sleeping on a hard wooden floor. Tonight it felt like heaven. We slept soundly with no more disturbances throughout the night.

When I awoke, the reverend was adding more wood to the stove. Peter was the only other one awake. He was sitting with his back against the wall, watching the reverend.

I wondered what his problem was. Why didn't he like me? I thought about all my friends at school. I was a really likable guy. I was certain that it wasn't my fault. He was the difficult one! Still, it bothered me that he didn't seem to want to be around me.

We talked and played simple games to pass the time during the day. The reverend brought us a few books to read. Jenny and I took turns reading aloud.

The sky was dark with heavy clouds all day. By late afternoon, Dad felt that it was dark enough to continue on. We left the church and immediately headed for cover in the nearby woods. The heavy layer of pine needles on the ground formed a green carpet that did not leave footprints.

We had walked several hours when suddenly a strong smell wafted up and filled my nose. I could hardly breathe. The others smelled it too. We all stopped in our tracks.

"It's coming from over there," called Dad. "Let me go check on it."

Dad slowly approached a giant oak tree. He squinted, trying to make out the object lying beneath it. He returned to where we stood waiting for him.

"It's just a dead skunk," he reported. "Let's keep moving."

We walked in a big circle around the tree to

avoid any further odor. We didn't get far, however, before Peter suddenly stopped.

"Listen!" he called nervously. "I hear barking!"

"Oh, no!" cried Mrs. Douglas. "The slave hunters have set the bloodhounds on us!"

By then I could hear the unmistakable sounds of dogs barking. I couldn't tell how far away they were, but I knew they weren't far.

"We've got to think fast," Dad said. His voice was thick with fear.

The barking was getting closer by the second. We were all beginning to panic. Liza started to cry. Nate was clinging tightly to Peter.

"We've got to find that skunk!" called Mrs. Douglas. She headed back to where the dead skunk had been.

"What are you doing?" cried Dad as he followed behind her.

"Just follow her!" Peter insisted.

Mrs. Douglas ran like a deer, clutching Liza close to her chest. Peter and Nate were right behind with my family in the rear.

Mrs. Douglas spotted the skunk. She continued running about a hundred feet into the thicket of trees. She stopped in front of a large oak tree.

"Quick, climb that tree," she ordered our

family. She pointed to the tree next to the oak.

Then Mrs. Douglas grabbed on to the oak tree and started climbing. Liza held tightly to her neck. Peter and Nate quickly followed their mother.

Jenny, Mom, Dad, and I climbed the tree next to the one the Douglases had climbed. Jenny missed a step and started to cry out. Mom steadied her and pushed her forward.

The smell of the skunk was so strong now that it burned my nose and eyes. I tried not to open my mouth to take a breath. I was afraid of tasting the smell too.

Finally we reached the top of the tree. We heard the dogs running in our direction. Three men on horseback were following them closely.

"I think they found something!" one of them yelled loudly.

6

A Confrontation

Between the stench of the skunk and my racing heart, I could barely breathe. I glanced at Mom. The terror on her face scared me even more. I was holding on to Jenny's leg to make sure that she stayed firmly planted on the limb above me.

A Confrontation

The dogs were near the tree where the skunk lay. They were circling the tree and barking wildly. One of the men rode closer to see what the dogs had found. Before he reached the bottom of the tree, he jerked the horse's reins abruptly. He turned the horse back around to leave.

"What is it?" the second man yelled. "What did they find?"

"It's a dead skunk!" the man yelled disgustedly. "Get your dogs away from that thing! They aren't going to be able to smell anything else all night!"

— The second man quickly rode ahead to the dogs. He called them away. At first they would not give up their barking. They continued to circle the tree. Then the man whistled loudly. The dogs followed the men as they rode away.

We stayed in the trees until we were sure they were far away. Then we climbed down swiftly. We tried to stay as far away from the skunk as we could. After we had a few minutes to recover, we started back through the woods.

We walked until we felt we could walk no more. Then we pushed ourselves to keep going. Finally, we were exhausted and ready to find somewhere to rest.

Dad felt sure that we were miles from the nearest town. The few farmhouses we had seen from the distance couldn't be trusted as safe houses. The temperature had warmed a bit from the day before. But it was still too cold to sleep without shelter. We were going to have to find our own shelter.

We discovered an old abandoned barn. Dad declared that it would have to do. It was not going to be much in the way of shelter. Part of the roof was missing. Some side boards were broken out too.

Dad and Peter worked to close up as many holes as possible. I helped the girls gather up some old hay. We picked the warmest corner of the barn and covered the floor with the hay.

Once we were settled, our stomachs reminded us that we had not eaten. We pulled out all the food that we had in our pockets. We had three apples, a chicken sandwich, some hard bread and cheese, and two handfuls of nuts that we had picked up along our way.

We divided the food as best we could. Peter quietly refused his portion. At first I was going to refuse mine in turn. After a moment, though, my hunger got the best of me. I ate an apple.

I was never really warm enough to sleep

soundly. At one point, I sat up to see if there wasn't some other way I could get comfortable. I noticed immediately that Peter was missing from the group.

I crept quietly out of the barn. Peter was sitting under a tree. He saw me but he didn't speak.

"Are you okay?" I asked quietly.

"Don't worry about me," he answered rudely.

At this point, my tired, hungry, aching body got the better of me.

"What's wrong with you?" I demanded.

He stared at me blankly. He didn't respond.

"Why do you hate me so much?" I cried. "Our skin is the same color. We're about the same age. You and I are exactly alike."

"We may both have black skin," he said angrily. "But we are not the same!" His eyes were cold and hard. He continued to stare me down. Finally, his anger broke through. He began to shout at me.

"You don't know anything about having to work in the fields until you can't stand anymore! You don't know how it feels to have a master's whip across your back! You don't know how it rips out your heart to have your papa sold and taken from you! You don't know how hard it is after your papa isn't there anymore! Then you have to look out for your mama, little brother, and sister. We are nothing alike!" he said with disgust and stormed off.

He was right. Our lives *were* very different. And he didn't have any idea how easy my life really was!

He thought I had been born free in Pennsylvania in the late 1830s. The reality was that I had been born nearly 150 years later. Not only was I free, but I lived in a modern world. And I had all the conveniences that went with it.

Suddenly my mind flashed back to Christmas at Grandma's just a few days earlier. I thought of the DVD player that I had insisted on having just because my friends had one. I remembered how it had seemed so crucial that I have that chemistry set. Suddenly I was ashamed to be me. When had I lost track of what was really important?

I decided not to follow Peter but to let him have time alone. I knew he would come back because of his family. I sat under the tree, waiting for him to return. After a long while, he reappeared. He walked directly to the barn. I stopped him before he could go inside.

"I'm sorry, Peter," I said sincerely. "You're right. I should have thought about all that."

"You just don't understand," he said. His voice broke. "Why is it that you were born free and I was born a slave?"

He turned his back to me and began to sob. It was as if all the pain and humiliation he had ever suffered was upon him all at once. I felt helpless. Nothing in my life had ever made me feel this bad. I couldn't even imagine it.

"What's happened to you isn't fair," I said quietly. "We both know that. But don't you see that's why I'm here? I know it isn't fair, and I want you to be free. That's why I'm here—to make sure you are."

His sobbing began to diminish out of complete exhaustion. He looked embarrassed as he wiped his eyes dry. When he was ready, we walked back into the barn together. Silently, we found our places on the floor.

Within minutes, I heard his breathing grow heavier. Soon I knew he was sleeping. I slept restlessly for a few hours. I kept dreaming that I was a slave with a cruel owner who worked me until I could not stand.

7

A Close Call

About midafternoon, Dad decided we should
move on. The sky was overcast, and it would be
dark soon. We packed up our things and moved
on without anything to eat.

This time when Dad offered, Peter allowed
him to carry Nate. Although he was still quiet,
Peter didn't seem to be quite as angry.

Jenny was in one of her talkative moods. Mom was constantly hushing her. Liza was humming softly with her head resting on her mother's shoulder.

"Aren't you guys hungry?" I finally asked.

They all agreed that they were.

"Then why is everyone in such a good mood?" I asked. My voice was filled with the frustration I felt.

"It's Christmas Eve, silly," Jenny replied. "Did you forget?"

I *had* forgotten. I hadn't even thought about Christmas at all. It lifted my spirits as well. It sure wouldn't be our traditional Christmas, but it was still Christmas. Jenny tried to quietly sing a Christmas carol, but Mom silenced her again.

About an hour later, we came to a wide stream. We had crossed over several frozen streams already. But here the water was flowing so fast that it had not frozen.

There were rocks to cross on. But they were not flat rocks. They were jutting up out of the water in all kinds of odd shapes. This was going to be a challenge!

We agreed that we would cross slowly, taking our time. Peter hoisted Nate onto his back. He said they would go first just to show us how easy it would be. Sure enough, Peter stepped from rock to rock like an acrobat on a high wire.

Peter called for his mother to come across. She followed his path. Mom crossed next. Then I followed close behind.

It wasn't as hard as it had first appeared. But I still had to concentrate on the slippery rocks beneath my feet.

Jenny carefully worked her way across behind me. Bringing up the rear was Dad with Liza on his shoulders.

Soon I reached the other side. I headed for the walnut tree I had spotted crossing the stream. I was hoping I could find some walnuts and have a little snack. It had been a long time since that apple for dinner last night.

I was searching for nuts when I heard a loud splash. I turned around just in time to see Jenny's head slip under the water. In a second, the water was washing her downstream.

Dad had Liza on his shoulders, so he couldn't catch Jenny. Mom and Mrs. Douglas began to scream. They ran along the edge of the stream in a desperate attempt to catch her.

Quick as a light, Peter set Nate down. Peter ran ahead along the edge of the water. He jumped from one rock to another. Soon he had reached the middle of the stream.

Jenny was only a couple feet away from him.

He stepped into the waist-deep water and grabbed hold of her drenched woolen coat. He pulled her up on a rock to sit and catch her breath. She was crying and shivering from the icy water.

Dad handed Liza to Mom and quickly reached Jenny. She clung tightly to Dad's neck as he carried her back to the edge of the stream. We quickly gathered around her. Everyone wanted to see that she was all right.

Suddenly, Dad looked up and said in a choked voice, "Oh, no! Not now!"

I turned around to see what he was looking at. I gasped in fear. A white man stood at the edge of the trees. He was dressed in a coonskin cap and bear coat. And he was holding a shotgun!

We must have made too much noise when we were screaming for Jenny. The slave hunters had heard us. I looked around. There was nowhere to run.

But then we stared in disbelief. The man laid his gun down on the ground and ran to us. We stepped back, not sure what he was doing.

"We've got to get this girl warm right away!" he shouted. "You have just a few minutes or she'll be deathly ill."

He quickly grabbed Jenny from Dad. He wrapped his heavy bear coat around her.

"Follow me back to my cabin," he called over his shoulder. He stopped briefly and picked up his shotgun.

We were so stunned that we didn't know what to do. We did know that he had Jenny. We had no choice but to follow him.

My mind was racing at this new turn of events. What was he going to do with us? Would the Douglas family be sent back? Would we be taken south and sold as slaves?

We entered a clearing in the woods to discover a large cabin. It was completely surrounded by dense trees. There was smoke coming from the chimney. It gave the cabin an almost cozy appearance. Could this be the home of a slave trader?

The man threw the door open wide as he entered. Then he beckoned us to follow. I could feel the warmth inside the cabin. I wanted to just collapse on the floor, absorbing the comfort of real shelter.

"Hattie, come quickly!" he called. "We need your help right away!"

An elderly, pleasant-looking woman appeared immediately. She wiped her hands on her apron.

"My goodness, Jacob," she said. "Where'd you find all these folks on such a cold day in December?"

"You wouldn't believe me if I told you!" he laughed. "But this one here fell in the creek. She needs tending to right away."

Jenny's wet head was sticking out of the big bear coat just enough for the woman to get a glimpse of her.

"Oh, my goodness!" Hattie exclaimed. "We've got to get her out of those wet clothes!"

"I don't believe she's the only one that's wet either," Jacob added.

Peter had been quietly shivering on the way back to the cabin. He was drenched from the waist down.

Mom pulled Jenny close to the fireplace. She ordered us to turn our backs while she took off Jenny's wet clothes. Immediately Hattie appeared with a soft flannel nightgown for Jenny. It was so big that it wrapped around her three times.

Mrs. Douglas watched the new strangers carefully. She carried Liza and Nate closer to the fire. They were both shivering uncontrollably. I wasn't sure if it was from the cold or the fear. They had that same fear in their eyes whenever they were around white people.

"Come here, young man," Hattie said to Peter. "I can give you some of Jacob's britches. I know they're not likely to fit properly. But they're still better than the wet ones you're wearing."

Peter hesitated for a moment. Then he slowly took the pants from her. He moved into a corner to change clothes.

"Come here, child," the woman said to Jenny. "I've got some soup to warm your insides."

Suddenly Jenny started crying and clinging to Mom.

"No!" Jenny shouted through her tears. "I'm not going to eat any of your food!"

"Why, child," the woman said softly. "What is the matter with you?"

"Get away from me!" screamed Jenny. "I know you're going to take us and sell us as slaves!"

"Goodness sakes alive, child!" Hattie said in amazement. "What put a foolish thought like that in your pretty little head?"

Jacob and Hattie stared openly at all of us now. They finally began to realize what was going on.

"Now look here," Jacob said sternly. "I don't know anything about selling anyone for slaves."

None of us moved or spoke. I guess he realized he would have to do more convincing than that.

"The only thing I know is that I came across some folks that were in trouble down by the stream. It appeared that someone fell in the water," he said. He looked at Jenny and smiled. "Luckily, I came across them just in time to help. That's all I know."

He looked at Dad. "Where are you folks headed to way out here?" he asked.

Hesitating, Dad told him we were on our way from Ripley to Cincinnati.

"Well, you've gone farther north than you were probably planning," he chuckled. "You're probably about eight or nine miles north of where you think you are."

"I must have gotten off course," Dad said. His voice was filled with frustration.

"Don't worry," Jacob assured him. "You're not so far off that you can't get there in a day."

"You folks gather by the fire and get warm now," said Hattie. "You're safe here. No one is going to bother you."

I could feel the weight lift from my shoulders. We had not been captured by slave hunters. Instead, it felt as though we had stumbled into the presence of angels.

8

A Christmas to Remember

Jacob and Hattie did their best to make us feel comfortable. They assured us that they were thrilled to have company. They said they didn't get many visitors.

"Most times we spend the entire winter without seeing another living soul. Having folks come to visit on Christmas Eve is a special treat," gushed Hattie.

It was obvious that we were indeed welcome. Hattie never sat down. First she made sure that everyone was warming up around the fire. Then she busied herself with feeding everybody. She served hot bowls of soup with crusty homemade bread.

"Mama, I'm still hungry," cried Nate after the first bowl.

"Shush now, Nate," Mrs. Douglas said.

"Oh, please let the child have some more," insisted Hattie. "I've got plenty."

Mrs. Douglas watched warily as Hattie filled Nate's bowl once again. It was plain to see that Mrs. Douglas still did not trust Jacob and Hattie. She was not sure that their intentions were honest.

"We'd best be getting on down to the cellar now," said Mrs. Douglas when we had finished eating.

Jacob looked at her in astonishment. He shook his head slowly from side to side.

"Mrs. Douglas," he said slowly. "When we invite guests into our home, we don't ask them to sleep in the cellar. Hattie and I will find warm places for all of you to sleep."

"But—but—" she stuttered. "It isn't safe."

"In all my life, I've never seen a slave hunter in these parts," promised Jacob.

"Mrs. Douglas," Hattie said, "you are welcome and safe in our home."

"I'm very grateful to you both," said Mrs. Douglas slowly.

"Besides," said Jacob, "this is Christmas Eve! We need to celebrate!"

Hattie pointed at the Christmas tree. "Isn't it beautiful?" she asked proudly. "Jacob brought it in just yesterday. He found it growing up on the hill behind the cabin. Why, he even helped me string the berries and put on the red satin ribbon."

"Jacob and I like to sing Christmas carols around the tree," she continued as we gathered around the tree. "Tonight it will be like we have a whole choir!"

It felt so good to laugh and sing again. Soon Liza and Jenny were dancing around the room. Nate clapped and cheered them on.

Then Jacob announced that it was time to read the Christmas story. He asked if Peter or I would like to read it for him. Peter immediately dropped his head and looked at his feet. I knew instantly that he could not read.

"I'll do it for you, sir," I answered quickly. I read

the story with only the light from the fireplace.

Afterwards, everyone was exhausted. Jacob and Hattie went to work gathering bedding for everyone.

"You children can sleep in the loft," Jacob said. He pointed to the sleeping loft. There were planks on the cross beams of the cabin. They formed an open balcony. Against the wall was a ladder to reach the loft.

I watched curiously as Jacob took hot bricks from the bottom of the fireplace. He placed them in a bucket and carried them up to the loft. He was back down shortly, declaring everything ready.

When we reached the loft, we found five pallets of soft sheets and quilts. I pulled back the covers to climb into bed. Then I discovered what Jacob had done with the bricks. He had carefully wrapped each brick with a heavy towel. Then he had placed them in between the sheets so we would have warm beds. We removed the bricks and climbed into our warm sheets.

"Thanks for offering to read the story," Peter said quietly when we were all in bed. "I didn't want to admit I can't read in front of everyone."

"It's okay," I said. "We all have things we can't do. I didn't want to admit I didn't know how to chop wood."

"Slave children don't get to go to school," Peter explained quietly. "We just work. We work all the time. But I'm going to learn to read when I get north," he said confidently.

"I know you will, Peter," I encouraged him.

I awoke the next morning to the sound of Jacob coming in the front door. There was a cold draft that followed him in. I had dreamed that he had been coming in and out of the door over and over again. Each time he had let in more cold air.

We climbed down the ladder from the loft. I discovered that I hadn't been dreaming after all. Jacob had been in his workshop preparing surprises for Christmas. He had placed colorful gifts at the bottom of the tree. In place of wrapping paper, he had used colored cloth tied with string.

Jacob very slowly handed out the gifts. He waited to see the look of joy on each face before he would move on to the next gift.

He gave all three of us boys wooden flutes that he had carved himself. They were carved with perfection and made a clear, rich sound.

Then Jacob gave Liza and Jenny their gifts at the same time. He asked them to open them together. They both tore into them and found two beautiful homemade dolls.

"Look, Mama! I have my own baby!" shouted

Liza gleefully. She jumped up and down, squealing with delight.

"Those are beautiful!" exclaimed Mom. "Did you make those yourself, Hattie?"

"Yes." Hattie smiled. "It gives me something to do during the long winter months. When spring comes, I take them to town and sell them."

Liza ran to Hattie, throwing her arms around her neck. She hugged her with such force that Hattie nearly toppled over. It was hard to know who was happier—Jacob and Hattie or the children with their first Christmas gifts.

Mrs. Douglas finally understood that Jacob and Hattie's generosity was sincere. She began to soften toward them.

Hattie cooked a mouthwatering Christmas dinner. It was second only to Grandma's cooking. Afterwards, Jacob declared that he had another surprise.

"Put on your coats," he ordered. "We're going outside. We had fresh snow last night."

I grumbled silently as I followed the group outside. I had looked forward to being out of the cold today.

"I dug this old sled out of the barn last night," he said, smiling. "I thought you young ones might enjoy taking a ride."

"A sled!" exclaimed Jenny. "Come on, David. Let's try it."

We pulled the sled up an embankment near the cabin. The Douglas children looked on warily. I realized that they had probably never ridden on a sled before.

I climbed on behind Jenny. We sailed down the hill. By the time we stopped, Nate was calling for his turn.

"Try it, Peter," I offered. "You can sit behind Nate like I did with Jenny."

At first he hesitated, but soon Peter was sailing down the hill. He and Nate whooped and hollered.

I wished that Peter could come back home with us. Then he and I could go sledding with my friends. I knew they would have liked Peter.

We took turns sledding until we were too cold to continue. Back inside, Hattie had warm apple cider waiting for us.

Late in the afternoon, we were sitting contentedly around the fireplace. Mrs. Douglas dug deep into the pocket of her dress. She pulled out some folded pages of a book. She handed them to Jacob and asked that he read them for her.

"What have you got here?" asked Jacob curiously. He carefully unfolded the pages.

"They're pages of the Bible," Mrs. Douglas said proudly. "My sister Charlotte learned to read. She always read to us in the evening. When I said I was going to run, she tore out these pages and gave them to me. She said she knew them by heart anyway."

Mrs. Douglas rocked slowly in the rocking chair. She smiled with her eyes closed. She listened as Jacob read each page.

When he finished, he asked that we stand and hold hands in a big circle. Mrs. Douglas hesitated for just a moment before slipping her dark hand into Jacob's white one. Then Jacob asked for blessings upon us as we continued to travel. It was the end of a wonderful Christmas day.

I kept staring at the smiling faces of the Douglas children. This day had been very special for them. They were happy with the little things I took for granted every day.

I worried about what would happen to the Douglases when we left them. I was frustrated because I would never know for sure that they had reached Canada. I only knew that I wanted them to reach freedom more than anything I had ever wanted in my life.

9

A Chance Meeting

We tried to say our good-byes hurriedly. We knew they would be painful to say. There was no point in dragging them out. We left that evening and planned to reach the outskirts of Cincinnati by sunrise. Then we'd hide out until that night.

Because we had gone farther north than planned, Dad figured we were safer from the slave traders. But we still did not feel completely safe. So we traveled in silence.

We reached the outskirts of Cincinnati right before sunrise. We decided to stay hidden at the edge of the woods until dark. Then we would go in search of Mr. Douglas.

It was a long day. It was hard to be quiet for so long, but we could not risk talking. We took turns napping throughout the day. The ones who stayed awake kept guard.

Later in the afternoon, we planned our entrance into the city. Mr. Douglas had given instructions to meet him after dark behind a warehouse. It was close to the railroad station. We would follow the tracks into the city. They would lead us to the warehouse.

We waited until it was completely dark. Now there were only a few people moving about. We crept quietly through the darkness. We were mindful of every little noise we heard.

There were several doors along the back of the warehouse. We were afraid to knock, so we just kept walking by. We kept as close to the building as possible.

As we were about to pass one of the doors, it suddenly opened a few inches. "In here!" a man whispered.

My heart was beating wildly as we entered the darkened warehouse. Once inside, someone lit a candle. Three black men stood before us. They stared at us in confusion.

"Percy!" exclaimed Mrs. Douglas. She ran to hug one of the men. "I knew you'd be here for us. I knew it!"

"Charity," he called softly as he hugged her tightly.

"Papa!" called Peter, Nate, and Liza in unison.

Tears came to my eyes as I watched the family reunite with their father. I was so happy for them—and for us. We had done what we had set out to do. We'd helped slaves escape on the Underground Railroad. I felt as if my heart would burst.

"Charity, where have you been?" asked Mr. Douglas. "Who are these folks? I thought you were supposed to be with Mayme Taylor."

"These are my friends," said Mrs. Douglas proudly. "It was on account of them that we made it this far."

"I'm grateful to you then," said Mr. Douglas.

He shook hands with Dad and me. He smiled and tipped his hat to Mom and Jenny. Then he reached to hug Mrs. Douglas once again.

"This here's Jake and Harper," he said. "They're going to help us get on the train to Columbus. Then there's a man who'll meet us in Columbus. It won't be long now. Soon we're going to be living free in Canada," he said, smiling broadly.

We continued to talk and share stories of our adventures. Suddenly there was a soft knock on the door.

"Get back in the corner and hide," demanded Jake quickly. "I'll take care of it."

Jake opened the door only a few inches and whispered quietly. Then he opened the door wider as three more people entered the room. Again a candle was lit. This time it revealed a young man and woman in their early twenties and an older woman.

"Come in, Harriet," said Jake warmly. He embraced the older woman. "We've been expecting you."

We stepped forward as Jake began making introductions. First he introduced the two young runaways from Alabama. Then he placed his arm tightly around the older woman's shoulders.

"I'm proud to call this lady a friend of mine," he said. His smile stretched from ear to ear. "This is Harriet Tubman."

I could hear Mom gasp in the darkness. My mind raced back to the stories that Mom had read to us. She had told us about Harriet Tubman's daring missions to carry slaves to freedom. I remembered that Harriet had been born a slave in Maryland. She had been called Moses by her people because she had led so many to freedom. In fact, she'd made over 17 missions, delivering more than 300 slaves to freedom.

"I'm honored to be your friend, Jake," Harriet said humbly.

We introduced ourselves one by one. I actually shook hands with the grand lady. We had never dreamed that we might actually meet her. To be in her presence was overwhelming.

She stayed only long enough to get something to eat and rest for a few minutes. Then she insisted that she had to go south once more. She said she had promised to go back for another family.

Harriet said good-bye quickly. Then she slipped back out into the darkness on another mission of freedom.

We spent only a few more minutes visiting. Then Dad said we needed to leave too.

"We have to be on our way," he insisted. "I really do hate to leave, but it's time to start back."

"You're going back?" asked Mr. Douglas in disbelief.

"It's hard to explain," said Dad. "But we have to go back."

Mr. Douglas hoisted Nate onto his shoulders. He walked over to Dad.

"I owe you a big debt for what you've done for my family," he said. He shook Dad's hand.

"And thank you, Mr. Tom, for carrying me," said Nate shyly.

"You're mighty welcome," Dad said. He smiled as he pumped Nate's hand up and down until Nate laughed.

Mrs. Douglas went to Mom and hugged her tightly. Tears fell freely.

Liza realized what was going on and ran to Jenny. She grabbed Jenny around the waist and rocked back and forth.

"You can't go now," said Liza. She sobbed into Jenny's coat. "I won't let you go."

Jenny started crying too. She bent down to give Liza a kiss on top of her head.

I walked to Peter and shook hands with him. I tried not to look him in the eye. I was afraid my emotions would get the best of me.

"Someday soon I'm going to be free like you," Peter said proudly. "I'm going to learn to read and write too. And when I do, I'm going to help other people be free—just like you did."

I swallowed hard. I hoped that would clear the huge lump from my throat. It was one of those times when being a guy was hard. It would be embarrassing to let anyone see me cry. But I felt like crying because I knew I would never see him again.

I also didn't want to say anything mushy and look stupid. But I wanted to let him know what a great person I thought he was. I was amazed at everything he had survived already.

After an awkward time of battling with myself, I raised my head. I looked him straight in the eye and paid him my highest compliment.

"I wish you were my brother," I said softly.

He looked at me in surprise and smiled widely. In that moment, we were brothers.

10

The Kindness of Strangers

We left the warehouse and made our way out of the city. We walked a few hours in complete darkness. Luckily, it was another dark, cloudy day. We hoped it would be safe enough to keep moving. We had to get back to Mayme's on time.

Dad kept us closer to the Ohio River this time to make sure we stayed on course. As a result, we were constantly listening for any sound of a stranger.

We walked all day. We only stopped twice to rest. By late in the afternoon, we were worn-out. I had never walked as much as I had in the past few days!

Darkness was falling again. We began searching for a safe place to spend the night.

From the direction of the river, we heard a bell ring softly. It rang two times. Then it paused and rang two times again.

"I think I know what that is," said Mom, smiling. "I read that there were people who stayed along the river after dark and rang a bell. It was a signal for any runaway slaves that it was safe to cross the river."

"Annie, are you sure?" questioned Dad. "We wouldn't want to come across the wrong people."

"Let's just sneak over there and see if we can spot anybody," I suggested.

"Yeah," Jenny added. "They might help us."

Dad was still not convinced. But he did agree to investigate the bell. As we neared the area, the bell continued ringing.

"Look out on the river!" Mom said excitedly. "There's a boat!"

Halfway across the river, a small boat was moving swiftly and quietly across the water. I could only make out one person in the boat.

When the boat reached the shore, someone stepped out of the darkness. He helped pull the boat onto the riverbank. The two men quickly secured the boat and moved away.

They neared our hiding place. Dad said softly, "Kind sir, we are friends of a friend."

Immediately they both stopped and turned in our direction.

"Show yourselves," one of the men ordered.

Bravely, Dad stepped out in full view.

"My family and I are seeking shelter for the night," Dad said calmly.

"Come with us," one man answered. We immediately fell in line behind the two men.

We didn't travel far before a house came into view. The familiar lantern hung in the window. The man approached the door and knocked only once. His knock was quickly answered.

"Who's there?"

"Friends of a friend," he said clearly. The door immediately opened.

All of us were quickly ushered into the cellar by a warm and friendly young white couple. Once the runaway from the boat was settled, the bell ringer left.

Dad greeted the nervous runaway. "My name is Tom Smithers."

"Mine's Henry," said the little man. He was visibly shaking now. Dad wrapped an old blanket tightly around Henry's shoulders.

"Are you okay?" Mom asked. "Are you sick?"

"I'm just sick with worry," Henry said quietly. "I know what my master will do to me if he catches me."

"You're safe here," Dad promised.

But when the couple came down the stairs, Henry bolted to a dark corner of the room. The couple seemed to understand his fear. They stayed only a few minutes. They explained that they were expecting someone to arrive early the next morning to help Henry to his next stop.

After the couple left, Dad coaxed Henry from the corner. We told Henry stories of our trip from Ripley to Cincinnati.

"You're in a safe house," explained Mom. "A station of the Underground Railroad."

"I heard tell of such things," Henry said in disbelief. "But I never thought there would be anybody to help me."

Henry ate hungrily. It was as if he had not eaten for days. When Jenny and I insisted we were full, he ate our leftovers.

Finally our bodies were exhausted. We settled down to sleep for a few precious hours.

Much too soon, we heard the cellar door creak open. A young white stranger appeared.

"My name's Ben," he introduced himself. We eyed him suspiciously. "I'm here to take Henry to a farm outside of Columbus. From there his contact will be Joseph."

Henry looked at Dad and Mom. He searched their faces for advice on what to do.

"How do you plan to safely deliver this man?" Dad inquired.

"I have a wagon loaded with hay," Ben explained. "The wagon has a false bottom where Henry can hide."

Dad nodded at Henry. Henry moved toward the cellar door.

We followed the two men out. It was the middle of the night. We watched as Henry climbed into the bottom of the wagon. The slats in the boards gave him plenty of air to breathe. With the hay stacked high, he was completely hidden. Feeling that he was safe, we headed in the opposite direction.

It was windy and bitter cold. It was the kind of day best spent indoors with the heat turned up. As we trudged along, I tried to imagine myself back home, warm and snug in front of the television.

About midmorning, we reached the same barn that we had stayed in before. Dad felt it would be safer to rest until darkness fell again. Jenny and I were exhausted and quickly agreed.

We slept through most of the afternoon. When I awoke, my stomach was growling fiercely.

"I'm going out exploring," I declared. "Maybe I can at least find some berries or something."

"Don't go far," warned Mom. "Stay within sight of the barn."

I made a circle around the barn. I couldn't find anything edible. Now I was frustrated and even more hungry. I made a little wider circle away from the barn. Finally I spotted a walnut tree.

I made my way toward the tree. Suddenly I felt a movement behind me. Out of nowhere, strong arms appeared and grasped me tightly around the waist. I screamed and struggled with all my might, but I couldn't break away. I tried prying the hands apart, but the grasp only tightened.

I struggled to turn myself around so I could see my captor's face. I couldn't get a good look at him, but I heard his evil laugh. That's when I knew for certain that I had been captured by a slave trader!

11

Captured

"Let me go!" I screamed. "Let me go!"

I was terrified as I struggled to free myself. I continued to try and wrestle myself away. Then another man stepped out of the trees.

"I got him!" yelled the man holding me.

"You caught a good one," he said. He smiled a wicked smile. "That boy's going to fetch a good price."

I continued screaming until a hand clapped tightly over my mouth.

"Let's gag him!" yelled one of the men. "I don't want to listen to him!"

Together they slipped a dirty rag over my mouth. They tied it tightly behind my head. I continued to fight as they tied a rope around my hands.

"It's too late to cross the river now," said one of the men. "Let's set up camp for the night."

They held on to the ropes tightly. They pushed me forward as we walked to the river's edge. Then they shoved me roughly against a tree. My back was pressed hard against the rough bark.

They wrapped the ropes several times around my chest and legs. I could no longer move. I knew that my chance for escape was unlikely.

"The boy's not going anywhere," they agreed.

Helplessly, I watched the two men as they went about setting up camp. My despair was growing by the minute. Where were Mom and Dad? I had to hold on to the hope that they would be able to rescue me somehow.

But what if they didn't? Would I actually be sold as a slave? And what if I didn't make it back to Ripley on time? Would I be trapped in the 1800s forever? I struggled again against the ropes. It was no use.

The men prepared their food and ate. They didn't offer me anything. I was disgusted to hear them laugh and talk about how much the highest bidder might pay for me at an auction. How could anyone sell someone else?

Tied to that tree and helpless, I thought of Peter. I remembered how he had tried to tell me about being owned by another person. I thought of how he had cried from the pain and humiliation he had suffered. And, finally, in those moments, I began to really understand.

The men were soon asleep and snoring loudly. Several long, cold hours passed. I was more afraid than ever that Dad and Mom would not find me. The fear began to overwhelm me. I shivered from the cold and the terror that gripped me.

Just as I was giving up hope, I heard a soft whistle. Relief flooded over me. It was the flute that Jacob had given me for Christmas. Dad had been carrying it in his pocket.

Then I saw Dad's shadowy figure moving just a few feet away. In just a minute, he was at my side. He whispered in my ear.

"Don't make a sound, David," he said softly. "I'll have you free in just a minute."

There was that word *free* again. It had never sounded so sweet.

Dad worked quickly and quietly to untie the ropes. Silently, we disappeared into the woods. The men were still unaware of my escape. We traveled in silence for about a mile. Then Dad stopped and threw his arms around me.

"David!" was all he could say as he pulled me closer.

"I'm all right, Dad," I managed to whisper.

"Let's keep moving," he said, wiping away his tears. "Your mom and sister are waiting for us."

We continued to weave our way through the woods. Finally we came to the hiding place. Immediately Mom and Jenny were hugging me and crying. We talked for only a few minutes and then moved on.

We covered a lot of ground before daylight. This time Dad said no more traveling during the day. It would be much safer to travel with the cover of darkness. I didn't argue with that.

We searched for a warm place to rest during the day. But by daylight, all we had found was a dark, dank cave.

In frustration, we huddled on the cold, damp floor. We had just gotten settled when we heard a noise at the entrance. I felt my body stiffen with fear. My mind immediately raced back to the two men.

We looked up. There stood a large black man. He was well over six feet tall. He was staring curiously at the four of us.

"I saw you folks entering the cave," he said in a deep voice. "I know a better place. Come with me. I'll show you."

We were desperate to find a warm, dry place with some food and water. We followed him out of the cave and into the woods. He moved noiselessly through the trees. He stopped occasionally to listen for any unusual sounds. After a few minutes, we arrived at an old abandoned cabin.

The door creaked as the man pushed it open. He took a look inside before entering. We waited for him to motion us forward. Then we quickly slipped into the cabin.

The cabin looked as if it had been abandoned many years ago. But it was strongly built and offered good shelter from the cold.

"There are some blankets in that cabinet," the man said. He pointed to the wall. "Bring them out. I'll get you something to eat."

We followed his directions. We wrapped ourselves in so many blankets that it was hard to walk.

"I've got this wild turkey," he said. He opened a cloth bag. "It's cold, but it's mighty good."

I was starving. I didn't care if it was cold or not. Grabbing a piece of meat, I stuffed it into my mouth.

The man unwrapped a cloth to reveal a loaf of hard bread. Then he set out a bucket of water.

"There's a spring with fresh water close by. I brought some if you're thirsty," he said. He offered Mom the cup.

The man stood near a window. He watched closely for any movement outside.

"Who are you?" Dad asked with his mouth full of bread and turkey.

"Name's William," he said in that deep voice.

"I was just wondering if you're real or an angel," Mom said.

He laughed quietly and said, "No, ma'am. I'm no angel. But I am looking for the promised land. Just like you folks, I reckon."

"How did you know about this place?" Mom asked. She gulped down her second cup of water.

"I found it yesterday," he said. "It looks like it's been used as a hiding place before. It doesn't feel safe, though. I was watching out that window all night."

"Are you heading north today?" Dad asked. He wiped his mouth with his sleeve.

"I'm waiting for my brother," he said nervously. "He's supposed to meet me around here. But he hasn't showed up yet."

Dad offered to help William keep watch. But William insisted that we get some rest. I went to sleep quickly but tossed about restlessly.

I dreamed about standing on an auction block with people surrounding me. They were bidding amounts of money to buy me as their slave. One man was poking me in the ribs with his cane. He was making me move around so bidders could get a better view.

The stabbing in my side increased until I began to wake up. As I tried to open my eyes, I saw a dark figure looming over me. Immediately, I panicked. I screamed and threw off the blankets so I could run.

12

Home, Sweet Home

"Calm down, David," I heard Dad saying. He grabbed my arm. "It's okay. It's just William and his brother."

Reality began to hit me now. Slowly I realized where I was. My heart was still beating wildly. I tried to recover from the terror of the dream.

Dad thanked William. William and his brother left the cabin. We watched as they disappeared into the woods.

Dad assured us that we could easily make it back to Mayme's by morning. The thought of some food and warmth got us going. We trudged out into the cold night air and began the final leg of our journey.

We walked steadfastly through the night. We picked up our pace a bit as we began to near Ripley. Dad had been right. We reached Mayme's house right before sunrise.

"Well, for goodness sake!" Mayme said with delight when she saw our faces at her door. "Come on in the house. Quickly now," she insisted. She practically pulled us into the kitchen.

"Now if that don't beat all!" she exclaimed as she looked us over. "Safe and sound and none too worse for the wear it appears."

"But starving to death," Jenny said. She moaned and rubbed her stomach.

"Well, child, I'm going to fix you the biggest breakfast you've ever had," Mayme said. She smiled as she set to work.

"Can I help?" Mom offered.

"My goodness, no," said Mayme. "I've made that trip before. I know how hard it is. You're going to need plenty of rest for a few days. Besides, traders have been roaming the area all week long. You'll be safer if you go down into the cellar."

We descended the creaky stairs once more.

"I hope I never have to see another cellar after this," I whispered to Mom. She smiled knowingly and nodded in agreement.

Soon we were wrapped in warm woolen blankets. Mayme came down the stairs with an enormous stack of pancakes and maple syrup. She returned with a platter of bacon and eggs.

Mayme perched herself on top of a barrel. She asked us to tell the whole story from the beginning. She was amazed at our good fortune of finding Jacob and Hattie and spending Christmas safely with them.

Mom told about safely delivering the Douglas family to the warehouse where Mr. Douglas was waiting. She was also quick to tell Mayme that we had met Harriet Tubman. Mayme was truly astounded by this. She said she looked forward to someday meeting the remarkable lady herself.

Then it was my turn to tell of my capture and escape from the slave traders. Mayme listened intently to my story. Her eyes crinkled with concern.

"Of course, I gave them quite a fight," I bragged. I was feeling much braver now since I was safely away from them. "Why, it took two of them to hold me down so they could tie me up," I added hurriedly.

"I can tell that story is going to get bigger every time it gets told," Dad said, laughing.

"That's all right," said Mayme seriously. "That boy had a rough time of it. If he wants to glorify the story a little bit, I reckon he's earned the right."

I smiled and thought of how much Mayme reminded me of Grandma. Then thoughts of home came flooding back. I'm ready to go home, I thought to myself. I am definitely ready to go home!

The trip had been a great vacation. But I sure wouldn't have wanted to live here permanently. I couldn't imagine living in fear all the time. And I sure missed the comforts of home. I was exhausted from the cold and the traveling and the sleeping on hard floors. My life back home sure was easy compared to this!

I thought about Peter again. He *had* to live his life here. He had no choice. I hoped that life would be better for him in Canada.

After breakfast, we were so tired. Mayme said she would make sure things stayed quiet and safe. We were to nap as long as we wanted. Dad, however, insisted that she wake us at 6:30 p.m. on the dot.

I awoke later to find Dad moving around the room restlessly.

"What's wrong, Dad?" I whispered.

"I think she should have come for us by now. It must be getting close to 7:00. I'm going to go upstairs and find out for myself," he finally declared.

"Okay," I mumbled and rolled back over to sleep.

Suddenly Dad was running down the stairs and shouting for us to wake up.

"Get up! Get up!" he yelled. "It's five minutes to 7:00!"

Immediately we all jumped up. We threw blankets everywhere. Jenny grabbed her doll. I clutched my flute. We bounded up the stairs. Mayme stood wide-eyed, watching us in shock.

"Thanks for everything!" Dad shouted. He darted past her.

"You've been wonderful," added Mom. She quickly brushed a kiss on Mayme's cheek.

"Bye," Jenny and I called. We dashed full speed out the back door.

"Run to the spot!" Dad yelled. "It's over there." He pointed. We ran as hard as we could. We were terrified that we would miss our return time and be stuck here forever!

We stopped directly on the spot. We were sure it was the right place. Nothing happened.

"Oh, Tom," Mom said breathlessly. "We've missed it."

Immediately there was a loud whoosh. We were caught up in a bright tunnel. We were traveling without moving our bodies. The familiar bright colors flashed around us. We felt ourselves magically transported.

There was an intense feeling of relief when the movements stopped and we found ourselves in the time machine. Grandma was staring at us through the window. Her hand was on the door handle. She opened the door wide and beckoned us out.

"Oh, Grandma!" Jenny and I exclaimed.

"We almost missed the ride!" I added. "We were asleep only ten minutes ago!"

Then everyone was talking at once. After quick hugs, we went straight into the house. Grandma's familiar warm kitchen had never felt better to me. A freshly baked chocolate cake stood in the middle of the table. We sat down immediately and got to work on it.

"You've got to tell me everything!" said Grandma excitedly. She poured large glasses of milk for everyone. "I can't wait to hear all about your trip."

I sat quietly, listening to the stories.

"David, you've been so quiet," Grandma noticed. "Tell me something about the trip."

"It was just amazing," I said thoughtfully. "Being there and meeting Peter and his family has just made me feel different about everything."

"How so?" she asked.

"I don't know if I can explain it," I said. I thought about the past week. "I guess it's just that I found out how important my freedom is to me. And I realized how easy I have it. I have lots of things to be thankful for—especially my family."

"Sounds like you did some growing up while you were gone," Grandma said.

"Yeah, I guess so," I answered softly.

"Do you think Peter and his family made it to Canada?" Grandma asked me.

"Oh, yes," I answered confidently. "I'm not sure how I know, but I just know they did. That's what made our journey on the Underground Railroad worth the trip."